THE **BELL** IN THE **BRIDGE**

THE **BELL IN THE BRIDGE**

Ted Kooser

illustrated by Barry Root

CANDLEWICK PRESS

CHARLIE WAS LONELY. Each summer he visited his grandparents' farm for two weeks while his parents went on a vacation. His grandmother was always busy cooking or cleaning, and his grandfather was always fixing machinery or driving his tractor. Charlie had to spend most of his time by himself.

Almost every day he played along a stream that ran through the valley. Sometimes he caught tadpoles and put them in a tin can to see if he could see them growing their legs, and sometimes he'd catch a baby turtle and try to encourage it to walk in the direction he wanted it to walk. It was hot and buggy by the stream, but anything was better than sitting in the house waiting for something interesting to happen.

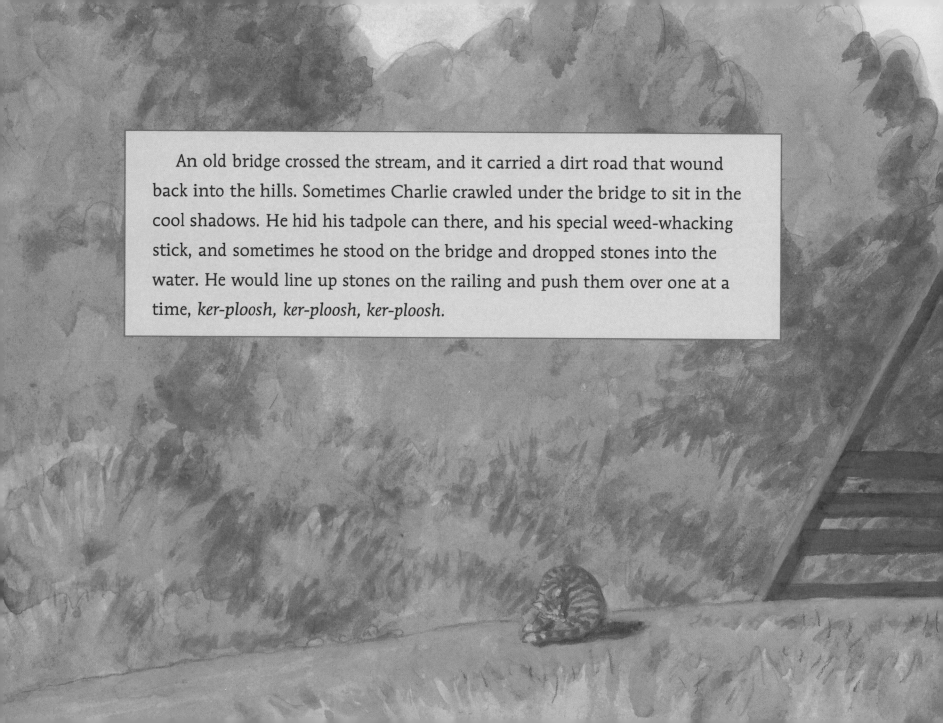

An old bridge crossed the stream, and it carried a dirt road that wound back into the hills. Sometimes Charlie crawled under the bridge to sit in the cool shadows. He hid his tadpole can there, and his special weed-whacking stick, and sometimes he stood on the bridge and dropped stones into the water. He would line up stones on the railing and push them over one at a time, *ker-ploosh, ker-ploosh, ker-ploosh.*

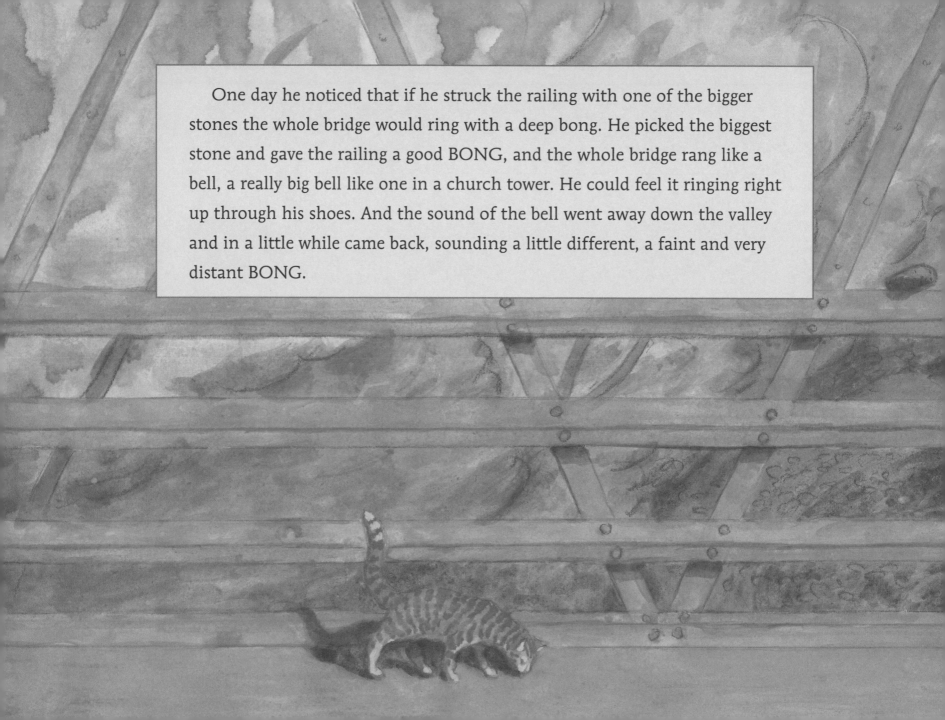

One day he noticed that if he struck the railing with one of the bigger stones the whole bridge would ring with a deep bong. He picked the biggest stone and gave the railing a good BONG, and the whole bridge rang like a bell, a really big bell like one in a church tower. He could feel it ringing right up through his shoes. And the sound of the bell went away down the valley and in a little while came back, sounding a little different, a faint and very distant BONG.

Charlie knew that the answering sound was probably just an echo, just the sound of his bell bouncing back from the other end of the valley. But one day when he struck the bridge and the echo came back, he heard, just after that bong, another one from far in the distance. He tried it again, giving the bridge a good blow with his stone, and in a little while the echo came back. And then there was the second sound, just like the first time.

That afternoon he told his grandmother what he had discovered, but she said Charlie was probably hearing the echo of the echo. Sometimes, she said, an echo will bounce back and forth for a long time, repeating and repeating, until the sound dies away into silence.

But Charlie was pretty sure that the extra bong that he was hearing was the sound of someone answering his bong with their own bong. It was quite a mystery, and there is nothing better than a good mystery when a person is lonely and bored in the middle of summer.

So every day, Charlie went out on the old bridge and rang it with a big stone he kept hidden in the weeds. It was just the right size for his hand, which he started calling his special bridge-ringing hand. And he called the stone his special bridge-ringing stone. Sometimes there was just one sound that came back, like an echo, but now and then there would come rolling back up the valley the other sound, too, like this:

BONG. . . . . . . BONG. . . . . BONG.

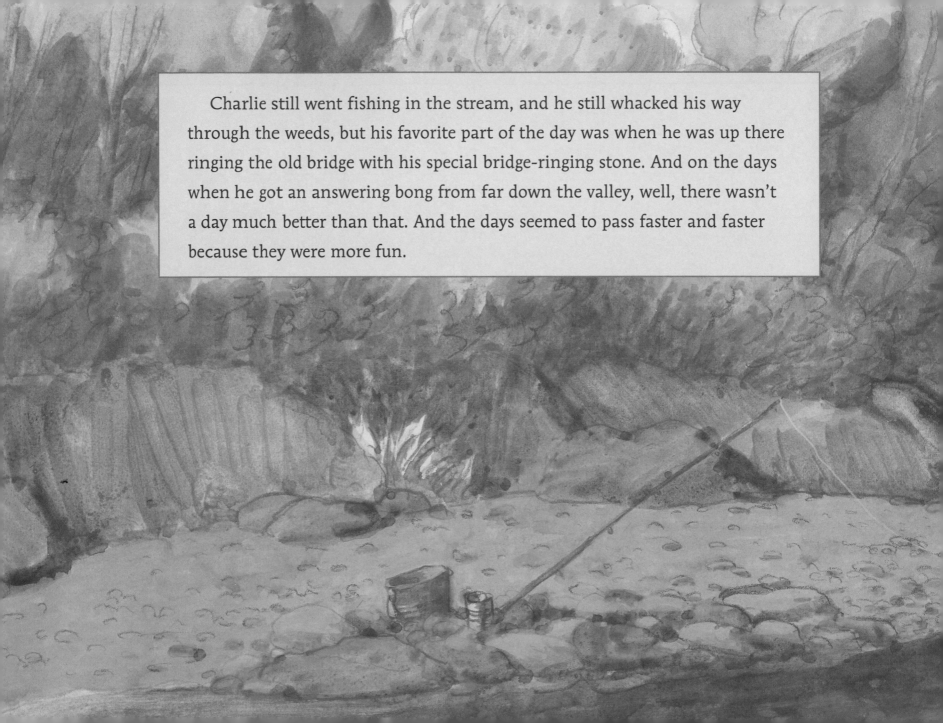

Charlie still went fishing in the stream, and he still whacked his way through the weeds, but his favorite part of the day was when he was up there ringing the old bridge with his special bridge-ringing stone. And on the days when he got an answering bong from far down the valley, well, there wasn't a day much better than that. And the days seemed to pass faster and faster because they were more fun.

At the end of the visit, Charlie's parents came to take him back to the city. While his father was packing things into the car, Charlie took his mother by the hand and led her out onto the bridge to show her what he had discovered.

Charlie said in an almost-whisper, "I'm going to give the bridge a bong, and sometimes you can hear the echo, and sometimes you can hear another bong from far away." And he bonged the bridge.

"Oh, my!" said his mother. "That's really loud!"

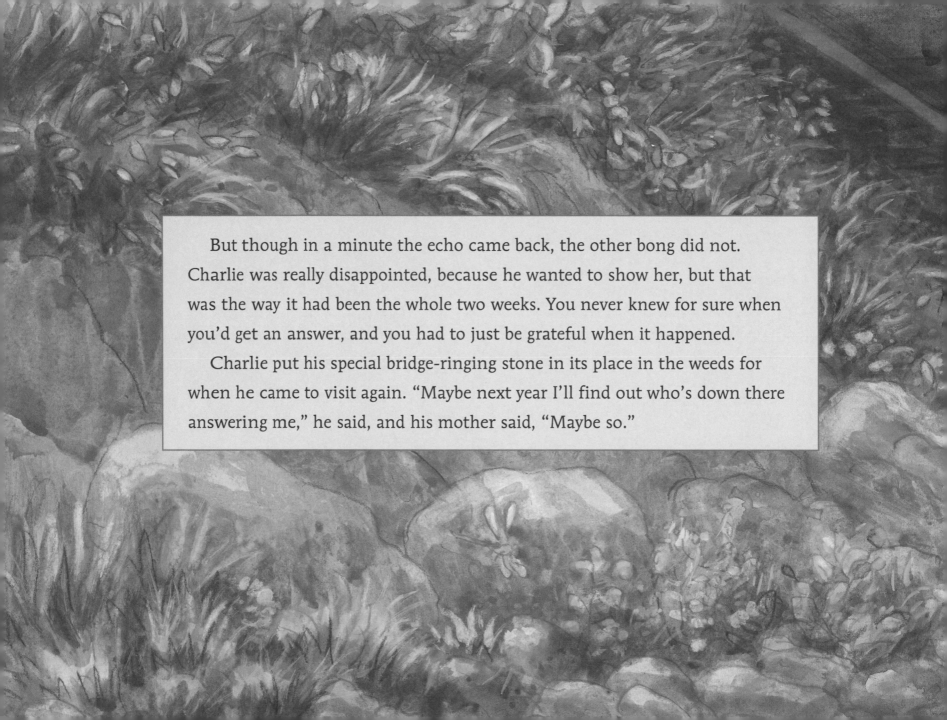

But though in a minute the echo came back, the other bong did not. Charlie was really disappointed, because he wanted to show her, but that was the way it had been the whole two weeks. You never knew for sure when you'd get an answer, and you had to just be grateful when it happened.

Charlie put his special bridge-ringing stone in its place in the weeds for when he came to visit again. "Maybe next year I'll find out who's down there answering me," he said, and his mother said, "Maybe so."

Then Charlie and his mother and father said good-bye to his grandparents, who said they were sad to see him leave, and they drove away down the valley. Now Charlie felt sad to be leaving, and his mother noticed and said, "Is there anything you'd like to do before we leave the valley?"

"Well, yes," said Charlie. "If you see another bridge along the stream, could you stop for just a minute?"

And sure enough, about a mile and a half from his grandparents' house, there was another bridge, much like the one he knew so well. Below it the stream was just a little bit wider, but the tall weeds and everything else were pretty much the same.

"Let me out for a minute!" said Charlie, and his father pulled the car over. Charlie jumped out and ran out onto the bridge, and what do you know?

There on the railing was a stone. It was just about the size of the one he'd been using, and at the place it was resting the bridge looked as if it had been bonged again and again, and the stone itself was a little scuffed and chipped, as if somebody had been using it to send an answer up the valley.

It looked like a stone chosen especially for that purpose. Charlie squinted and looked far up the valley, but he couldn't see anything but summer haze. And when he looked down, he saw footprints the same size as his, but the soles were of a different pattern. And he looked all around, but there was no sign of anybody.

Charlie gave the bridge a little good-bye bong, and the sound went up the stream and disappeared. He set the stone on the railing where he'd found it, and he and his parents drove away.

And just as they went out of sight around the bend, a boy about Charlie's age came up along the creek bottom and walked out onto the bridge. He had a special weed-whacking stick with him and a little frog in a jar. And he set down the stick and the jar and picked up the stone. And he gave the bridge a good blow with that bridge-ringing stone, and the noise went up the valley and disappeared into the trees. And though he waited a long time, there was no answer. "Maybe next summer I'll find out who's answering me," he thought. "I'd sure like to know."

To the memory of John and Elizabeth Moser
T. K.

For Emily Kang Bulcken
B. R.

First edition 2016

Library of Congress Catalog Card Number 2015934467
ISBN 978-0-7636-6481-7

16 17 18 19 20 21 CCP 10 9 8 7 6 5 4 3 2 1

Printed in Shenzhen, Guangdong, China

This book was typeset in ITC Mendoza Roman.
The illustrations were done in watercolor and gouache.

Candlewick Press
99 Dover Street
Somerville, Massachusetts 02144

visit us at www.candlewick.com